This Boxer Books paperback belongs to

. . . .

www.boxerbooks.com

To Gulliver and Rocket
and to all the little yellow birds
out there . . . especially Auntie Kate,
who was one of the best of them.

First published in Great Britain in 2011
by Boxer Books Limited.
www.boxerbooks.com

First published in the US in 2010 by Schwartz & Wade Books, an imprint of Random House Children's Books.
Published by arrangement with Random House Children's Books, a division of Random House, Inc. New York, New York, USA.
All rights reserved.

ISBN 978-1-907967-00-9

1 3 5 7 9 10 8 6 4 2

Printed in China

All of our papers are sourced from managed forests and renewable resources.

The author wishes to acknowledge the insight and support of Joan Kindig, associate professor of reading education
at James Madison University; and Jane Morrissey, kindergarten teacher, and Laura Hulbert, lower school learning specialist,
both of Brooklyn Friends School.

How Rocket Learnt to Read

Tad Hills

Boxer Books

Rocket loved to play.
He loved to chase leaves
and chew sticks.
He loved to listen to the birds sing.

Every autumn morning, after chasing leaves,
Rocket would lie down in his favourite spot under
his favourite tree. There he'd sniff the neighbourhood
smells and settle in for a good nap.

But one day . . . a little yellow bird startled Rocket.

"Aha! My first student! Wonderful!" she sang.

Rocket was confused. "Student? I'm not a—"

"But if I am your teacher," the bird interrupted,
"then you must be my student."

Rocket found it hard to argue with this bird.

"I am so glad you saw my sign!" the bird chirped.

"Oh, yes, I can *see* it," Rocket said. "But I don't know how to read."

"Can't read? Fantastic!" She waved a wing. "Welcome to my classroom."

"But I just came here to nap," Rocket said.

"No, no! There will be no napping in class," declared the bird.

"Except, of course, during naptime."

"Well, then, I can take a nap over here," said Rocket. "I've had a very busy morning."

"Not to worry, I'll be around every day," chirped the bird. "Until the weather turns."

class
starts
today

As Rocket breathed in the crisp air, the little yellow bird hung her banner. "Ah, the wondrous, mighty, gorgeous alphabet," she marvelled. "Where it all begins."

Opening up a book, the bird began to read. She sang out the story of an unlucky dog named Buster who'd lost his favourite bone.

A cool breeze carried her lively voice across
the garden. At first Rocket was disturbed.

But before long he found
himself captivated.

To Rocket the story was as
delicious as the earthy smells
of autumn. It was as exciting as
chasing leaves. He closed his eyes.

"'As Buster dug and dug under
the lilac bush,'" the bird read,
"'he felt something familiar.'"

Rocket waited.

Was it the bone? he wondered.

Silence.

"Was it the bone?"
he called to the bird.

More silence.

"WAS IT THE BONE?!"
Rocket shouted.
Suddenly he was
rushing to the tree.

"WELL,
WAS IT?"

But the little yellow bird was gone.

The next morning Rocket arrived early.

WORD OF the day: DOG

At last the little yellow bird appeared. "Hello!
How wonderful to see you in class," she chirped.
"I can tell by your waggy tail that you are well rested."
"I'd like to hear the end of the story, please,"
said Rocket.

"That seems like a fine way to start the day," chirped
the bird. She gave Rocket a name tag and began to read.

Every day Rocket
returned to the little
yellow bird's classroom.

In the morning the bird
taught him a new letter,

until he had learnt all
of the wondrous, mighty,
gorgeous alphabet.

Together they sang out the sounds that each letter makes and spelt the sounds they heard around them.

With a G and many Rs they spelt Mr Barker's growl.

GRRRRRRRRRR!

They spelt the sound of the wind, which was growing colder by the day.

WHHOOSSS

HHHHHHH...

Soon they were spelling words, like G-U-S-T for the grey and windy time of year, and R-E-D for the colour of the leaves.

And each afternoon the bird read a story. She read stories about dogs and birds. She read about leaves changing colours and about birds flying south for the winter.

Then one day the weather turned and the letter banner disappeared.

"See you again in the glorious spring," the bird sang.

And as she flew into the wintry sky, she called, "Don't forget! Words are built one letter at a time!"

The days grew shorter, and
the leaves fell from the trees.

The grass became crunchy.
Soon Rocket's classroom
disappeared under the snow.

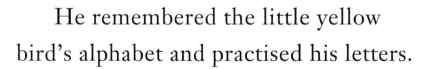

He remembered the little yellow
bird's alphabet and practised his letters.

Rocket thought about the bird's sweet chirp while he sounded out words

like D-I-G

and W-I-N-D

and C-O-L-D.

He made new friends and spelt their names.

"Hi there, F-R-E-D.

"Hello, E-M-M-A."

He spelt everything.

S-U-N.   M-E-L-T.

When Rocket spelt M-U-D, he knew that spring, as it always does, had returned.

The breeze blew warmer, the grass grew greener
and a sign appeared.

Early the next morning, Rocket rushed to his classroom.
As he waited, he spelt W-A-G.

Soon the little yellow bird arrived. "Aha! My star student!" she sang. "How wonderful to see you. I can tell by your waggy tail that you are ready for class."

Welcome Back, Rocket

Then together they began to read. They read stories about birds flying north in the spring. They read about picnics in the warm sun. And they read about Buster, the lucky dog who found his bone under the lilac bush.

And when they were finished, they read it again.

And again.

And A-G-A-I-N.

Enjoy more Tad Hills stories from Boxer Books

Duck and Goose

Duck and Goose find an egg. "Who does it belong to?" they ask. Duck says it is his because he saw it first. Goose says it is his because he touched it first. Little by little they agree that the most important thing is to look after the egg and decide to share it. But their parenting skills come to an abrupt end when a little bird tells them that their egg is really a ball. A delightfully funny story with rich paintings and strong main characters. Parents everywhere will recognise this tale of one-upmanship, which firmly establishes the positive aspects of learning to share.

ISBN: 978-1-905417-26-1

Duck, Duck, Goose

Duck and Goose are the very best of pals – that is, until Duck's new friend Thistle arrives. Thistle is good at everything (or so she thinks) from maths to standing on her head to holding her breath. Duck thinks Thistle is wonderful, but Goose is not so sure… In this charming and humorous tale, Duck and Goose learn that sharing your best friend isn't always easy.

ISBN: 978-1-906250-32-4

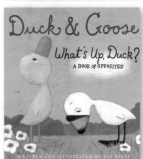

Duck and Goose: What's Up, Duck?

Little siblings of Duck and Goose fans rejoice! The stars of the best-selling *Duck & Goose* and *Duck, Duck, Goose* return in this fun-filled book, which introduces basic opposites. Goose carries an oh-so-heavy log, while Duck easily balances a light-as-a-feather feather. Thistle is one fast bird, but Goose is slooo-w. And when Duck is sound asleep, Goose is wide awake. With a simple text, colourful illustrations and lovable characters, this is a wonderful introduction to an important concept.

ISBN: 978-1-907152-05-4

Duck & Goose: 1, 2, 3

Duck and Goose return in their second concept book appearance! All the lovable characters from *Duck & Goose* and *Duck, Duck, Goose* return, this time to introduce basic counting concepts. One goose. Two ducks. Three friends. As the characters illustrate numbers from 1 to 10, children will love following the simple text and colourful illustrations. A fun-filled introduction to an important concept.

ISBN: 978-1-907152-06-1

Duck and Goose: How Are You Feeling?

Duck and Goose return in their third concept book appearance! All the lovable characters from *Duck & Goose* and *Duck, Duck, Goose* return, this time to teach little ones about feelings. The simple text and colourful illustrations will help children to identify familiar feelings like happy, sad, scared and proud. A simple and reassuring introduction to an important concept.

ISBN: 978-1-907152-07-8